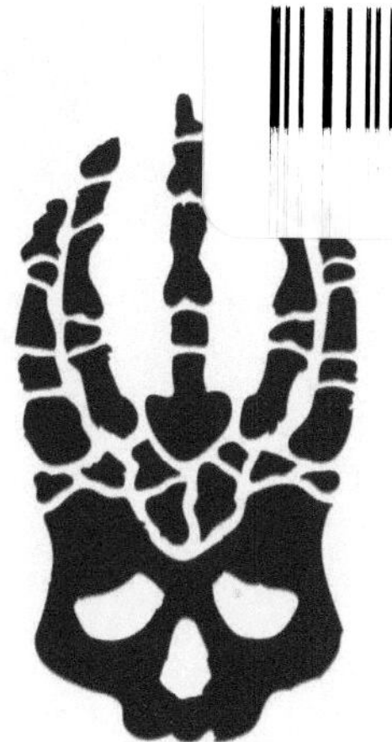

SKYBREAKER

TYLER J. WELCH

Asphodel Press LLC

Beaver Dam, Wisconsin | tylerjwelch.com

Skybreaker
Copyright © 2025 by Tyler J. Welch

Published by Asphodel Press LLC
Beaver Dam, Wisconsin
www.tylerjwelch.com

Library of Congress Control Number: 2025905930

ISBN 979-8-9905586-3-2 (paperback)
ISBN 979-8-9905586-4-9 (ebook)

Cover art, design, and interior formatting by Nicole Welch
Asphodel Press logo by Nicole Welch

First Edition: 2025
Printed and bound by IngramSpark

This novella uses instances of the Mayan language and certain truthful aspects of how and where the Maya people lived. It is purely a work of fiction and should not be read in a way that would incite readers to make any correlation between the Maya people and the contents of this story. The indigenous groups who call(ed) Mesoamerica home are extremely fascinating. They built beautiful civilizations, and I hold great admiration and respect for them and their history.

—Tyler J. Welch

SKYBREAKER

"The power of worship is unprecedented.
It is humanity's most sacred, and calamitous creation."

CHAPTER ONE

The seven Elders stand around their bleeding pit, under the ceiling of the lowest chamber in the Kan Temple. Orange rust hues of fire bounce the surrounding stone walls as if the floor were pooled in a shallow depth of water, or some other reflective liquid. This chamber is, at the moment, silent, as they await an answer from the god for whom they spilled their blood moments ago—their palms bleeding like crimson waterfalls while they ask for confirmation that their celestial calculations are correct. And if so, will this god they beseech, the Skybreaker, hear their call to come down from the heavens and save Earth from the coming darkness?

The will of the Elders is strong. For this is no typical eclipse they foresee in their calculations. As they see it, this is the tribe's centurion eclipse, the hundredth they will see since the start of recording. And like the others, this moon too will try blocking the sun's golden rays that give life to the land upon which they thrive. Only this time, they believe the moon must be stronger, having a hundred years of willful power stored, and great resentment held over its previous attempts to stick stubbornly in place affront the sun having been foiled by their sky god.

What the Elders do not know is that the Skybreaker they have so worshiped for these many years is not a god at all. This Skybreaker is not from the heavens at all, not from the Earth at all, not even something lost to the endless expanse of time, an entity long old and gone from here. What the dragon god of the skies is though—what is thought to have saved them every eclipse thus far by shoving the moon as it stops in front of the sun, keeping it again on its orbital course—is a creation of their own, one of deep belief and dire need as their fear of the moon permanently stopping the sun's rays afflicts them beyond any measure. And so, from that need, a god was born, many years long past. Before their calendar, their rise of intelligence, their greater understanding of what is possible and what is not. A fear and a story that birthed then and is ingrained in every new generation of Maya since.

A continued belief. Mostly out of fear.

The Elders hear a low, distant rumble far outside the temple's stone walls, a rolling heavy cloud high in the Yucatan's sky, the home of their Skybreaker. This is the Elders' faith misleading them however—a self-deception—as they expect an answer from the sky god, the entity for whom they bleed and from whom they seek answers. Though from the depths of the earth surrounding the temple is where the thunderous disturbance emanates, *not* the altitude of a flying benevolent beast affirming their reception.

A far different god hears them, one that has been in

slumber for eons, slowly feeding on the power of spilled Maya blood. Every drop the Maya people give in their many rituals for their many different reasons, is completely stolen in secret. The potency of each drink sinking down into the ground where this hidden evil quietly thirsts on the blood's power, patiently waiting for the day he has drank enough to rise and rain darkness down upon the Yucatan—then, the rest of the Earth in entirety.

He slumbers. And he thirsts.

And he waits.

And he beckons those above at times, tricking them into pouring more of their red life to what they think is to the Skybreaker and their other benevolent gods and goddesses. But it is always him, the oldest and vilest of the Ancients. The Dark One: the selfish, scheming, rotund, dark god of guile.

CHAPTER TWO

Cualli

Mother and Father went off this morning, after the rise of sun and eating together—off to the Kan Temple where those of age can meet with the Elders, pray, and seek guidance from the sun and sky gods. We worship the sky the most, as he brings us everything we need for life. He brings us rain. He brings drink for our crops and harvest foods. He brings us rays that save us from the darkness of night, rays that warm our faces, setting us afire with warmth and will for each day and season's cycle.

I wait for the seasons to start over again. Impatiently I wait, as I am not of age to visit the Kan Temple. But soon, it is coming; with the next new sun, I will be seventeen suns of age. Then, I will join Mother, Father, and others of our tribe as an adult, as an equal.

A stone flies over my shoulder and hides amongst the loamy soil—warmed already from the late morning skies—with an earthen thud. Balam's hearty laughter ensues as my head swings around, my hair dashing through the light breeze in a fair dance.

"My Cualli, where are you heading?" Balam laughs more while running and jumping over a thick patch of jungle floor towards me. "And without me? How are you to be mine if the evils of the world take you while out alone, without protection?" Balam jests with his handsome smirk.

His dreaded locks, beaded with ebony rounds and turquoise stones, fight the air like a ballet of spears, making for a gorgeous battlefield. The war is felt in my thighs and nicks my knees like the tip of a finely made arrowhead.

I raise a brow.

"And how am I to be yours if my heart and courage fall so short as to leave me in a paralysis, fearful of even the grass fields in search of morning berries—which of course are to be shared with such a man? . . . Or boy?"

He closes in now, catching me by the arm, handsome smirk still shining, surely glittering a reflection in my verdant eyes.

"Boy!?" he spouts. "I am as near as you, Cualli. With the new sun, we can kneel within the pyramids and temples," he says, "together even." With a wink.

I start on my way again; it is not wise for me to spend too long in his eyes.

"I'm off to the fields. Joining me? Or are you off with Aapo and the others for more hunt?"

"I am walking you to the fields. Then, I am leaving you to your own heart and courage."

"I accept this protection." I show a smile, and with the quick glimpse can see his bronze skin shining from the sky's growing fire as it beams down through paths in the dense maze of tree canopy. "Will it be to the west trees again this day?"

"It will. The boars are moving lots. It is their season for bearing, and we must follow the land's signs." He looks to the ocean above. I can tell he is in reverie and speaking thoughts to our gods and the Mother Earth. "It is the One Mother, the world, to whom we must kneel to and follow the most."

I say nothing. Though, I agree and find myself hoping that when the time comes—with the next new sun—he will choose me to walk his days with. His proud worship of the gods and the land make me wish for him to be mine in my adult and elder years. And the way the earth tremors up into my knees when he is near is an affirmation or, perhaps, a voice from the world itself, telling me of our paths being for each other. We walk together the rest of the way, stopping as we meet the field's edge.

"Here is where you must go, and I, with our courage," he says. "Aapo and the others will need me again this day."

"Hunt hard, Balam. Aim true!"

"Stay safe, my Cualli."

He bounds off, knotted locks again spearing the warm air in dance, and I meet the grasses underfoot. The smell is cleaner here in the southwest fields. Grasses and flowering fruits flow in the winds, the same currents the bees and colorful flies use to carousel themselves across distances. A screech from a distant high hawk pierces clouds that look to soon be overhead. I spend more time thinking of what news Mother and Father will bring back from the Elders than giving focus to my harvest. Still, I find enough grain and berries to aid in an evening meal, even after helping myself to their joy while I foraged. Two of the fruits I stash in a separate buckskin pouch for Balam. I take leave of the fields just as mid-sun approaches and clouds cast overhead, and as more of our women come to give their work of the land. A few give look on my leave; I wonder of their thoughts—worried they wonder what is of more importance than my time in the fields and gardens—procuring food for all the mouths, both young and old, of the tribe—but I wish to be back before Mother and Father's return, anxious to hear of theirs, and the other family leaders' attendance. Such news—mostly of the gods and celestial events—I always find enthralling in the most sacred of ways.

I make my way back home. The sight of the homes on the southern side brings me a sense of safety and familiarity—always. The mud-walled and stone foundations below grass and palm-pitched roofs scent the air, filling my adorned nostrils, letting me know where I am even if my sight were stolen from me. The coolness of the shade in our home is a nice easy break from the harsh light and heat outside. And the far off clouds move slowly this day, and have yet to reach over us.

Mother and Father are not inside, and the other houses here are quiet. The younger children are off in play, and I only assume most of our adults and those of age are too at the temple. I pick up the rough piece of jade I've been working into a glyph necklace. I'm no good at it but hope to someday be one of the best jewelry and lapidary workers we have.

I take the piece to a much larger stone for grinding and start the hard work of stone-shaping. The glyph-work that will be centered on the jade will be the most exciting part of the piece, but that is a way off yet. Hours of hard work remain before I should start such intricacies. It's really the part that keeps me going—the glyph-work—if I didn't have that to look forward to, I believe my progress would fall short and I may never finish, nor would I have ever finished the others.

The handwork is tedious *and painful*. It doesn't take long for rigidity and knotting to set deep into my knuckles and wrists, even my young ones, and just as I put the jade—which is quite nearing a proper circle—down, Mother's and Father's steps are heard, and I run out to meet their ritual painted faces.

It's so good to see them! The yellow of their smiles shows clear within the striking white paint across their golden Maya skin. I run to hug Father, the clattering of stone, shell, and wood adornments sound on our embrace.

He laughs. "Cualli, my daughter, why are you not in the fields?"

A sly embarrassment finds me. "Oh, I was, Father." My eyes go from his to the dry dirt beneath us. "My mind wandered nowhere but stuck to you and Mother and what news may come from the Kan Temple." I sigh, shoulders showing surrender. "I can see now my age is showing. If I were of age, such things would not find me so bound and tethered to simple curiosities. I see I have failed. I did bring back some harvest—though only enough for this evening's meal."

Mother's hand lies on my low shoulders. She is tall and strong. I should look up to and wish to be as grand as her, even though father gets most of my idolatry.

"Too hard on yourself, Cualli," she says. "Even the next sun will not bring you such discipline. Such a thing will take many more of our calendars. Fret not, you are well on your way."

"Your mother speaks truth. And having the gods, Elders, and Kan Temple held so strongly in your thoughts is not shameful, you should be proud of such a thing . . . Hold your eyes high to the sun and stars, Cualli, daughter of my Atziri," he says, looking to Mother.

I meet Father's face again, instantly finding admiration in his old sun-damaged eyes that now hold very little white. It's impossible to hide my returning smile. I thank him, "*Dios bo'otik*, Father."

He kisses my forehead. "Let us get inside. There is much to discuss, Cualli. The Elders say the grandest of eclipses is soon coming, and we will all be needed for a mass ritual to invoke the Skybreaker."

Excitement warms in my chest at the mention of the dragon as well as the eclipse—as it will be the first in my life.

"Before you take eyes to the ground again . . ." Mother says with a pause, ". . . the Elders have said we will need us all, including those who are not yet of age."

"Me as well?" I ask, a slight gasp happening. "The eclipse, the ritual, *I am to join?*"

Father tufts my hair, smiling. "You are to join, my daughter. We will need everyone for such a powerful event."

CHAPTER THREE

Cualli

I almost don't believe it, and staying still becomes difficult while Mother and Father prepare the evening's meal. *Is this real? Am I really going to be allowed to take part in this eclipse ritual, and why?* Something isn't adding up, and it strikes both excitement and worry in me—worry that my parents have misheard the Elders or that the Elders will find reason I will not be joining for the mass ritual.

"Daughter, sit." Father says as he takes to the ground near our hearth. "Mother is near finished mashing berries. Then, she will join us in circle."

"Yes, Father." I join him on the packed dirt within our home.

We always take silence and speak thanks together in circle before we eat. It is our Maya custom and is how we show our hearts to each other, and our gods.

Father takes my hand. "Cualli," he says, placing his and mine down atop my left knee, "take silence with me, Daughter. Give your heart and blood to the Skybreaker."

"Should we not wait for Mother?"

"She will understand," he says. "This is important. The

Skybreaker needs to hear from us all. He must have enough worship and blood to break the coming skies for us."

I sit and give silence as Father requests. But I cannot give the Skybreaker my heart—my attention—right now. I have far too many questions. Mother's steps near, and the sweetness of mash she brings with tempts my mouth into a tingle after my nose tastes it on the air. I keep my eyes closed in silence with Father, but I know Mother takes seat next to me, opposite Father—she takes my other hand in hers and rests it on my only available knee—to join us in ritual. I feel childish and weak again; my mind wanders in and out of everything except the one thing it should be resting on: giving attention and worship to Skybreaker. I worry too much.

"That is all we will give this evening," Father says. "We will continue our worship to him each passing day up to the eclipse, to show our need of him, and to grant him the power he needs to come down from the skies."

I open my eyes now. Our pottery lie before us with this night's meal—sweet berry mash, dried and cured boar from days prior, and a large bowl of grain. A sight and warm scent that would normally make my stomach yearn but tonight does no such thing.

"When is the eclipse, Father?"

He grins. I try to be stoic and plain, but it's clear he sees through. My nerves and excitement—my young heart—must show as bright as the celestial god in the summer sky of the dry season.

"Soon, Cualli. It is the next and coming moon that will be the one to block the day's light." He scoops berries and grain together in one hand; he often mixes foods that make little sense to me. I start with cured meat, then grain, and I'll save the berry mash for last. That way the sugars stay and do not get poured away with the other foods. Father swallows a gulp and continues, "Fear not. It runs fast across the skies, but we have the coming weeks to worship and prepare."

"Am I really to join?" I cast looks to both Mother and Father, left and right. "It is no trick of games?"

"No trick," says Mother. She starts taking evening meal as well.

I look to Father, for a sort of confirmation, even though Mother never lies. There are times I wonder if Mother is hurt by such things. I hope it isn't so, and there's part of me that wishes I could let go of the tightness with which I hold Father, to give more of that hold to Mother; it would bring us closer, I'm sure . . . For some reason unknown to me, however, it just doesn't end up happening. It's a fault of mine, I'm aware, and need to figure out and push through whatever barrier lies within me. I do not want Mother to feel absent or ignored.

Father nods an affirmation, his mouth full.

I continue eating and remain in my head. Father says, "Those even far younger than yourself will be part of the mass gathering, Cualli." His words slur and are choked away by the foods he continues palming. "You'll see, and it will be grand. The day's light will be blotted out by the moon, and that is when all our worship to Skybreaker will be counted. He will fly from the skies, and his shattering wail will push the moon back on its course, giving us the power of the sun once again."

"Will we see him? In the skies, Father?"

"If you look hard enough and believe strongly enough with your Maya heart, then yes, Cualli, I believe you may see his flight above."

"Truly?"

"It is only the Elders of the Kan that see his truth, but that is because they give all their heart and all their blood to his worship. If you give enough, Cualli, yes . . . you will see."

Mother's hand finds my knee again, and I am grateful. For now, even more nerves find me. *I hope to see him*! "Do all eclipses need such vast numbers of us, even those not of age?"

"This one is most rare," Father says with his mouth newly filled and nodding to Mother.

"This alignment brings an eclipse with a strength we've yet to see. It marks our one hundredth," she says as she pats her hand, still on my knee. "Father speaks true. A most rare moon this one is. Most Maya hearts never get a chance to view a moon this strong in its will to stop the sun's reach."

Father speaks again through his palmed food, "I am proud and glad that my daughter . . ." he grabs my left shoulder firmly, "and my Atziri . . ." he looks, raising brows to Mother, "are alive with strong beating hearts, to witness such a powerful moon and to aid in such a vital Skybreaker summon."

He smiles wide showing gratitude as large as the skies

themselves; Mother and I smile too, as his pride spills over us creating a circle of heart and entwinement.

"Tomorrow everyone is to take to the Kan Temple to choose a cutting stone. Mother and I already have ours from when we became of age. For you Cualli, this means a great deal and is a day you will always remember. For this is the stone you will always use when giving your blood to the gods. You and the others who are not yet of age will hand choose a stone that will be yours for your entire life, one that will even be buried with your mortal shell when death finds you."

"It's important you choose a stone that speaks to you," says Mother.

Father nods in a bow. "Mother speaks truth. Take care to find the stone that is meant for you. There is only one!"

I nod, hearing them clear.

"I will do just that, Mother, Father. I promise to make you proud."

Night comes—the stars and eventually the moon with it. I see most of the sky this night as it rotates with the passing of time, as sleep does not come; my mind far too steeped in the news Mother and Father brought with them. The disbelief has waned, like phases of a fast-racing celestial orb—at home in the blackness of the sky—but what remains is just as consuming. The Skybreaker, the eclipse, the cutting stone I am to choose, all fogging every other possible thought. Mostly though, it is Skybreaker himself—the dragon—from whom I cannot tear my mind. I wonder of his vastness. I wonder of his color, his shape, his power, and what sounds such a force could bring overhead. I wonder if he will accept me and my worship. Will I be worthy enough for him to hear my prayers and feel the blood and heart I give him? The thoughts move quickly, making it difficult to really grasp on and do anything constructive with them, which at times leads to frustration . . . spiking small tempers in my Maya heart.

Eventually the night meets its midpoint and with it comes Balam. Maybe planets will align and we will see each other at the Kan Temple tomorrow. The thought of choosing stones together—one of the greatest deals and proudest moments in a Maya's journey to adulthood—causes a percussion in my chest. A strong and near off rhythm beat of tribal drum.

I hope his hunt went well, and I look forward to hearing the tale. And more meat is always good fortune for us, all of us. With such a grand event on the coming horizons, many feasts will likely come too. As long as Balam hunted with strong will and heart, which I'm sure he did, the hunt will have been a success, another that will bring with it a story worthy of telling for many, many new suns.

My heart eventually settles; even a Maya heart can only beat so hard for so long before it comes to take a needed rest. Going back inside our home would be safer, but I now tire, and the wavering grasses in the night's breeze kiss my bare arms, thighs, and waist, slowing me down—down to the motion of the stars and distant gods and ancestors above who watch over us, insisting that I sleep.

And I am gone.

Gone, but alive, in another plane. Our dream plane. A new place this time, not the places I dream of most where it is I and Balam, or I and Mother and Father in the brightness of a warm day. No. Here I am alone, and it is dark. Sun has gone and so have the stars. The ground has gone; there is nothing on which my worn feet press, no solid and plain clay earth beneath, nor grasses, nor our thick jungle of trees. Even I have gone—as I look down for my legs, hands, anything of my mortal shell—but it does not share this dream. Only my *ch'ulel* has drifted here, leaving the rest behind.

A rumble, I hear it in the distance. But what distance? For it is all blackness here. I listen closely . . .

. . . I can hear my breath, though only faintly, as though my lungs and throat are away, away as far as those distant rumbles. Rumbles that sound like a quake of the clay and limestone that make the ground of our peninsula. Something large, something powerful.

The breaths grow deeper. I am no longer sure they are my own.

"*You, my life-blood . . .*" A dissonant abyssal voicing whispers in echo from below, "*I beckon you . . .*

"*Give, A—LL, to me,*" the rotund deepness adds.

My eyes squint, searching, peering, seeking what or who

lies in the expanse. Nothing. Nothing at all but black oblivion. I seek more deeply with my eyes; the breathing remains. I am still unsure if it is my own. I call out to the throaty echo that reverberated through the distance to my ears, but nothing comes; my own throat is not here; I have no voice.

I'm shunted from the depths, fast, like an erupting volcano spitting what it held in its infernal gut. And with that shunt comes the ire of morning sun, throwing its rays into my eyes, driving me to wakefulness.

I sit up with a gasp of dry, early hour air, darting my eyes, bearing myself. The open ground of warm-taupe-colored clay near the base of our highest pyramid—the Kan Temple—is my bed, and all around is nothing but the flat earthen clay. The surrounding grasses and temple are far enough off that only a raised yell would reach anyone at the barren's edge.

Coming first is a strike of panic as this is not where I had drifted into sleep. That was back home, just at the border of our guaya trees where I could still see the starlit sky as I laid. Though now, I am here in the barren. My chest drum beating strong against its encasement of ribs. A swath of heat pulses in my veins. My hand goes to my heart while I feel this comfort.

And I look, gazing to the sky in grand astonishment that the Skybreaker would pull me to his place, to speak to *me*. This is the grandest of gifts. I know now the truth of his power and know now what I must do. As the god, Skybreaker, needs me. His beckon, I shall heed.

CHAPTER FOUR

As the Maya people of the peninsula sleep, the dark god beneath the barren becomes increasingly aware of the numbers entering the state of dream. But Guile is a patient one, waiting until the deadest time of night to make his call. His steady, slow, deep, and calm gargantuan breaths resonate within his subterranean hollow—calmly readying himself for the pull. He pulls one by one, but so efficient he is that within minutes he has beckoned all the dreamers to his low plane where there is no light, little air, and no hope.

His dry mouth begins to salivate as he feels more and more Maya *ch'ulel* within his dreadful space, where he can feel the pulse of blood and the beat of their mortal hearts teasing his thirst for power and ascension. He has been sleeping far too long, and it is time for another reigning scourge across the entirety of Earth.

The grey-dusted stone that is the moon revolves around the blue-green orb he slumbers within, and is on course to cross the sun, and he knows this. He too knows the bodies above will succumb to fear and flock to worship and pour blood in the

Skybreaker's name. The blood and energy the Maya people put forth in their mindless venture will not go to waste however. It will feed something but not what they think. The dark god Guile smiles in his chambered casket of stone and clay. His pull is strong, and the bodies above sleepwalk their way closer to him—some heeding the call with more curiosity and will than others. Some, like the young woman Cualli, make their way nearly overhead, not knowing the ambitious and cruel Guile lies in wait, feeding them trickery on pretty silver-cast plates.

Cualli's feet patter lightly across the edge of the barren, unaware she has been pulled and displaced from her comfortable spot under her favored guaya trees. Everything is dark for her, and as hard as she tries, she sees nothing in the vastness of the dark plane. She hears him though . . . Hears him breathing and calling to her, asking for her to give him all she can. He asks for her blood and for her to kneel to him. He asks her to give all her energy and worship so he can come down from the blue-set skies and save her people from a permanent umbra. A casted sky that would last for days, months, years, forever—without his aid to push it away.

Or so she believes.

This is not the people's fabricated god of the sky. If only Cualli and the rest of her Maya tribe knew, oh, how things may have gone differently. And that is just one of the many unfortunate facets of this tragic story. If only they knew. But this is not the only time this story, or ones unmistakably akin to it have unfolded, or *will* unfold. This guise, this . . . guile, is played over and over again. Always created by humans. Fools they are. Unable to let the wind take their fear. So, they succumb to it. They let it eat them until they see no other choice but to create. Create the very thing that causes this history to continue on through the eons. Fools they are. Led by fear, and little else.

Cualli soon wakes with the turn of the Earth and firelight from the east. Her excitement is beyond measure; she feels atop the world and full of power. She can see the Kan Temple off in the distance at the other edge of the barren. She is full of life, sitting in one of the only dry, dead places within all the Yucatan—the clay beneath and around her encompassing nearly a square mile, holding nothing but the temple, the cracked scorched ground, and the fat vile thing slumbering below.

She is a flower in the desert right now, a pure joy in an ultimate sadness, a beat of life in a dry and evil void.

She runs off, her lightly calloused pretty feet sounding across the massive circle of clay within the lush tropical peninsula. A smile sits on her face, and a sense of purpose resounds in her chest. South she goes, back home to Mother and Father, leaving behind the barren—for now—and the dark god Guile, grinning in nefarious delectation.

CHAPTER FIVE

Cualli

I tell Mother and Father of my night and where my dreams took me. Mother grabs my face, both her hands resting on my perked cheeks. "Cualli, as did we! Father and I woke outside after the Skybreaker spoke to us, beckoning worship."

"A shared dream," Father says. "Many of us awoke outside. It seems Skybreaker pulled all our *ch'ulel* into his place, showing us he will need all our numbers if he is to come and push such a strong-willed moon for us."

Mother and Father's joy is all around. It's on their faces, in their yellowed smiles. It's in their hands, arms, the posture with which they walk the Mother Earth with. Mine, however, has sank. And I feel weak and selfish for it. Great happiness should course my veins that all the tribe was gifted such a godly visit. Though, my young heart falls with knowing it was not just I that was chosen specifically—singled out—by the god. The feeling of being chosen had granted a confidence and self-power that I never had experienced before. And as I find myself sinking away from such a thing, I miss it. I crave being the owner of that power again.

I pull from Mother's tender hold. "What does this mean then?"

Father answers, "It shows our Elders were very true and foresaw with great accuracy." He raises his old but mighty fist above his shoulder, clenching it like he's holding his own heart aloft, squeezing from it his blood to gift the gods. "The Elders' decision to include all the tribe, even those not of age, was the wisest of calls. The wings of the sky, the Skybreaker—he calls for and needs the blood gift from us all."

"He beckoned us all then?"

"This is truth you speak, Cualli, yes," says Father.

Mother notes the shallowness of my shoulders. "Cualli, this does not take from the weight of your own dream. Fear not, Daughter. Your grandness and power is not diminished. This shows we are all holding the strongest of hearts. It does not show that yours is of lesser value because it was not the only one beckoned."

Her eyes offer support, comfort, and understanding—but of actual help they offer little. And I know this is yet but another sign of my young heart; it makes me feel as if I'm a child.

"I hear you, Mother." I bow my head to her, showing respect and hoping to aid in my attempt to end and retreat from the conversion. "I am off now. The journey to choose my stone consumes me, and I wish to set out while the sun is low."

"Before morning fruits with Father and I?" she asks, a beckon of her own, heard in her soft voice.

"Atziri, do not bind her," Father says, standing tall and

putting his fist against his chest—showing pride. "Our daughter is showing her heart! She shows the importance of such a ritual by placing it above her belly, even if it brings with it an ache." He looks to me, no smile shown, but a creased brow and flared nose. I can see the flame behind the masculine look; Father is proud. I bring my hand to my chest, both in response to his words and to the comfort of heat in my veins once again.

Once again, I feel power within myself.

I take my leave from our mud-walled home, eyes set strong on the horizon line to the northeast. The still-rising to zenith sun blasts my brilliant and white—young—eyes. There is pressure in my walk. The richly moist and cool ground is dotted with short weeds, and the occasional thorned vine meets with my weathered feet. The possibilities of today's sun bring with it a smile across my smooth, golden face.

The walk back to the Kan Temple pyramid near where I awoke earlier is a long enough travel that the sun may reach its midpoint and highest summit in today's sky before I arrive.

The skies are clear. Blue. And without effort, my feet pat themselves against the land one after the other, one leading the next; they know where my heart destines.

Eventually, across the way, others making the same journey come into view. Several I recognize as peers of mine, other not-of-age tribe members that, like me, an exception has been made for. And farther out from them—across the way—more can be seen on the horizon's edge, too far to recognize by face or dress.

The smell of dense Yucatan soil and flowering vegetation

make my nose wrinkle as I breath in the heavy odors the sun bakes off the summer's fully lived flora. I look into the west wind, finding a flowering sac nicte tree in its full glory of orange sunburst cloud-colored petals, a deep and true sign of the dry season. Its perfume washes over me as I walk. I think of how gorgeous this land is—the beauty of this Earth, of our peninsula, it brings life into me and makes me never want to join my ancestors in death. Even if I am chosen, if my *ch'ulel* is chosen for a reincarnation . . . my memories of this life would not follow, and that has always felt inferior to having one life that could last into eternity. The flowers, the trees, my tribe, it all makes me never want to leave.

Hearty voices, deeper than my own and distant enough to be unclear, make me turn just in time to see a thrown rock closing in on me. I duck a step to the side—my right—and watch as it passes through the air where my shoulder had been a single breath before.

The hushed hearty voices take a less hidden volume as they turn into giggles, chuckles, and laughs.

"One of these times, you are to hit me," I say as I stand from my crouch, knuckles in my hips. "Then, oh, then, how are you to win over the drum in my chest if you are no longer able to take breath . . . by my hands."

As the tribe of young warriors emerge from the foliage line, the sounds of merriment turn to a chorus of young men playfully voicing opinions of loss towards Balam.

I stand true and strong; though, unknown to them, my

knees do not feel as strong as I'd wish on Balam's approach, which is a mere walk but looks like that of a hunter's and warrior's dance—one that I believe would tremor the Yucatan ground under any woman's foot.

Balam reaches me first. Aapo and the others are not far behind; though, they keep their place behind him some.

His quiet chuckle and keen smile meet me. "My Cualli, your heart and courage have not fallen short. Your stance," he says, placing a hand on the side of my thin upper arm, "and even your words hold a power that makes me proud to be seen at your side, even now.

"Your words, and their meaning, are heard. I will say that is the last stone my hands will throw over the shoulder of my Cualli."

I smile. "I was only saying such a thing in jest, Balam. The stones are fine . . ." I smirk up at him as I turn and continue my walk northeast. "As long as your aim doesn't falter, you will stay alive, I assure you." I offer a coquettish laugh to help him understand.

"No, your words speak true. Even I am not perfect in the gods' eyes. Falter I can, and I wouldn't wish its time to be on a meaningless stone meant only in game.

"That is the last of them. I give you truth," he finishes.

My smile grows; it can't be helped. The safety I feel around him only expands. I hope he is to choose me when the time comes. He keeps his pace with mine while we continue to the pyramid. The others are with us but still letting Balam and me have our own space.

"I am off to find my cutting stone."

"As are we. A grand day this sun has brought, and a grand night the stars gave us all as well."

"You dreamed too. I'm sure of it."

"Yes, Cualli, I dreamed of the Breaker of Skies. He asked for blood and worship, Aapo and the others dreamt the same, and worship and gift blood, we will. We must if he is to gain enough power to move the moon when it takes its stance."

"I admit I felt loss when I heard I was not the only one pulled to him while sleeping. And at that, I am ashamed."

"Cualli." He places his hand so that it lingers gently on my arm, "We are Maya. We seek pride and to be owners of heavy and strongly important hearts. Let your shame fall to the bowels of Earth. It takes strength to confess such, and for this, you should be proud."

"*Dios bo'otik*, Balam."

"Would you choose stones with me?" he asks.

I look behind us at the others. "Are you not going with them to choose?"

"I am asking you."

The exit of words becomes difficult, and I find myself hoping the choke is not apparent. Many new suns pass—years it seems—before their escape is made. "Yes," is all that makes it out. I hope the many passing years did not bring him to think of me as unsure. Balam turns to the others behind, back-stepping to keep beside me.

"Aapo, Cualli and I are to choose stones at the temple. Once we near, I ask you to leave us to do so. Stay with the others and await together. Choose strongly!"

Aapo and the others cast hands to the air and nod their acceptance. Part of me feels an intruder, my other, more proud part, doesn't care.

CHAPTER SIX

Cualli

The heat is as high as the sun; our gold skin glistens though there has been no change in pace. The pyramid and its steps get higher and higher on approach. This day will be the first we are able—allowed rather—to pass the surrounding flat earth of clay that gives buffer to the Kan Temple—what we call the barren. It brings me a joy and an unease, but an unease of excitement. I glance off to the west, I can see the scaled and cracked ground where I woke earlier this day.

The whole of this mass circle around the pyramid changes none-at-all, it's all the same scorched land of red-tinged warm-taupe clay that matches that of a serpent's hide. Even when our great rains come to us, this area before the temple remains ever parched. The cracked skin of Earth swallows every drop of blue, as if something below demands the soil to let it pass, feeding the core of Mother Earth.

"Are you still working that piece of jade you spoke of?" asks Balam, interrupting the reverie of my latest dream.

"I wish I was better. There's much to learn before I am any

sort of decent at the craft, but yes, I'm still working."

"Time brings with it many things, Cualli. Keep at it . . . It's sure to become a grand piece."

I can feel my cheeks warm even more, and I ask Balam, "Do you have any idea of what stones the Elders will have for us to choose?"

He tilts his head some, brows rising. "Ahh, likely that most will be chert or obsidian. Those work easily, and the peninsula is abundant with such stone."

"I'm sure you are right."

I know what Balam says is truth, and I knew what answer he would likely give. I knew already myself. Still I asked, hoping the mention of others. I do not want something so common for such an important and lifelong ritual item. I wish for something rare. In the least—not our common chert or obsidian of which we see so much.

"They are sharp," he continues, "And hold a strong edge. We will find the sharpest and most brilliant just for you, Cualli."

I smile his way and give his sharp shoulder an affirming and endearing jab.

As I look back to the north horizon, the stepped pyramid that is the Kan Temple stretches to the sky, towering over me. A flutter of pretty flies swarms my stomach, and I can feel Balam's pace strengthen. He must either meet the swarm in his stomach with an eager warrior's courage, or so balanced is his nature that such swarm pays him no visit.

The flies want me to slow, but I cannot show Balam any

weakness, and so I step larger, keeping at his side. The heavily jeweled and adorned Elders stand in a row beside a split and hollowed tree trunk—a hardwood chest filled with hand-knapped cutting stones. Many not-of-age, and nearing-of-age sit on the scorched clay, awaiting their turn to approach the chest and take their pick, hoping to find one that speaks clear and loudly to them.

Balam and I take seat amongst the others, yet we are still distant enough that I feel it is just him and me. He places his hand on my right knee. I am afraid to look him in his eyes; nerves take hold of me and play games within my skull. These are nerves of the good kind—bringing nausea that is charmingly pleasurable and unsettling all at the same time. My stare is ahead at the young boy choosing his stone, whose hair has yet grown to his thin shoulders, and whose Maya skin has yet to be etched with ink or symbolic scarification. I keep the stare while I bear myself through the dichotomic plague of nerves and rest my hand atop Balam's. My hand feels small on his stable ground, like a gentle elaenia bird standing on a grand plateau.

"He is so young," I say, hoping to break some of my own tension. And bring me back down to the earth.

"Young but full of pride, I am sure, as are his mother and father. His birth was lucky, bringing him here in time to bleed for the Breaker of Skies," says Balam. He adds, "His shoulders are small, but they are square and sharp. Look. He stands well, showing his might."

I look to him as he speaks; his words take me. His eyes

remain ahead watching the young boy as he walks from the Elders, holding a small obsidian knapped to a jaggedly sharp edge. The way Balam sits tall and finds pride in our peers, even this much younger boy, makes my heart feel him even more. The pride, honor, and courage he sees in everyone and not just himself, it strikes me as the truest a Maya heart can be. The way I see Balam's heart here, now, it is the kind of heart all of us wish to achieve and wish to show our gods.

I fall. And I yearn in this moment like I have not before. And the drum in my chest beats with a freedom from doubt.

He stands, not letting my hand fall away. "Let us go, my Cualli. There are stones calling to us."

We approach the hallowed trunk with the Elders standing at each side. The pretty flies are gone, off in the flowering fields now; my peace and station is strong and present at Balam's side. Deep veneration dotted with jealousy hits as we near the many Elders—their large lobes, adorned septums, pierced bridges, many new suns worth of glyphs and art inked across their worn bronze skin. The patience needed for such grand expression does not match my own. My young ch'ulel wishes to be so adorned—now not later.

The Elders are silent. The two eldest flank the chest and carve a path through the air with their hands, leading and offering us to take our turns in hearing what the stones have to say to us. We start sifting through the knapped pieces, doing so with a respect for each one. We go slow, handling some and palming them over in our hands, running our thumbs across the blade edge of those we think may be calling out to us. Most of them are, in fact, chert and obsidian. Though many of the chert have large layers of rusted yellows and some even show deep greens, most though are the familiar matte grey, and none of these speak volumes to me.

I see Balam move a few pieces of obsidian, and then, his hand stops, midair.

He smiles at me, with a wink.

He lifts what he has uncovered. A rough light-brown and orange stone with a knapped side that is the blue of a grand summer's sky. I hear no words from the stone, but it takes my breath in a short gasp.

He pushes his open palm closer to me, the chalcedony with its sharp blue edge leaving me lost for words—speechless.

"This one, my Cualli, speaks to me," he says as he grabs my hand and places it in mine, the smoothed edge of blue stone chills the inside of my soft palm. "And it says it is for you."

"But you are who found it," I say. "It should be yours!" And I nod to him as I try placing the stone back in his.

Balam grabs my hand, enclosing both of his around mine, trapping my hand and the stone in a warm cage of insistence. "It is for you, Cualli. I know it."

I can see in his deep brown eyes and high brows that his only intention is for this stone to be mine. I am lost for words still, but I accept and show him my acknowledgment. Balam is back in the chest of stones; I am holding my chalcedony in both palms, staring down into its beauty and rarity. I am taken aback that such a grand stone would even be in the collection for us to choose from.

Balam takes me from my escape into the blue skies of the stone's edge, "Look here," he says. "The edge of this is done very well. The hold is strong too." He isn't wrong. The stonework couldn't be better, and the hold matches his grip as if it was made by the Mother Earth specifically for him and no one else.

"It's just obsidian . . ." He tilts his head a bit, and his lips purse.

"No, Balam, it is more than that. It is your obsidian. You won't find another with such a hold and strong edge.

"You know it." I add with heart.

He smiles and grips the glossed black stone in his hand. "That is truth, Cualli. We have found our cutting stones. Today is a grand day," he says as he looks to the clear hot azure sky.

As we make our way back to the others—most in wait to approach the chest—Aapo calls over with a gestured hand in the air, catching our attention. I tell Balam to go. His warrior and hunter peers are wanting him to be a part of their day as well. I can tell he both wants to stay at my side and to go to them. But my persuasion wins, and he joins the others as I take my leave of the barren around the pyramid. I make my way back south to find some solitude in the fields, or under a favorite section of our tropic forest.

The fields come to near after hours have past and so too does my favorite dense tree line that canopies over a bed of soft lush, low grasses. The cool shade still appeals to me, but now that I am here, my mind runs. I think of the jade piece, still unfinished back home. An anxiety has built in me, and I know if I lay down in the shaded grass, staring into the vast sky, I won't be able to find the solace I came here for. My mind will be busy; I will want to heed the anxiety in my bones; I will want to move, do something active, do something that matters.

So, I turn home, and reach it soon enough. I grab my jade right away (Mother and Father are out) and put my hands and tools to use. My wrist, knuckles, even my elbows start to lock in ache, but the shape of the stone gets finished, and excitement carries me on and into the most anticipated part of the craft—the glyph work.

I start with light etching, to get main shapes and line work laid out on the stone. My hands feel as if they are in a stiff knot. I try shaking the knot out, pushing my fingers into my palms, cracking as many of the tightly wound knots as I can. My thumbs are always the most stubborn and painful to crack, but I manage to wring both of their tension, wincing a touch as I do.

The etch across the jade's face is our witz glyph to represent a mountain. The iconography called to me, making me think of how I am improving at igniting courage in myself, in my heart. Strength as well—I am proud of this self-ignition I've been able to raise within me. And it's important I do, as I need Balam to see. I need Mother and Father to see. I need myself to see that, whatever mountains present themselves, I, Cualli, can overcome with my courage and my strength.

CHAPTER SEVEN

Cualli

Mother and Father get home late—Father from helping clean deer and tapir from a grand hunt, Mother from harvesting in the fields with other women and children of the tribe. Mother shows love and adoration as she says, "That is fine stonework, Cualli. Wear it and be proud, Daughter." Father slides a mark across my face in play before smiling his age-stained teeth at me and taking his blood-soaked hands to the basin. Their acknowledgment warms my core, and Father's actions speak louder than Mother's words.

I sleep outside again this evening looking to the stars, admittedly hoping the Skybreaker will again grasp me into his plane. Only this time, I hope to see and hear more while there. I want to see more than the blackness of my last dream and hear more of his words. This makes sleep—yet again—difficult to fall into. My mind races sprints within a heavily leafed Yucatan Forest of thoughts, wishes, hopes, and desires.

. . . I realize the stars have successfully taken me though, for the early amber horizon—riding a vertical line harshly up into the endless heavens—is now what my weak and lazy eyes find. I lie, keeping the horizon a jutted staircase, and search my memory for a dream or walk with the gods that may be hiding in the vagueness that is last night's escape from wakefulness.

The scent of soil moistened by early hour dew and grasses beaded with drops of crystal bring a softness that helps me in my search; a calm mind tends to find paths, treasures, even memories more easily.

Though . . .

I find nothing.

And deep down I know such an encounter with the mighty Skybreaker would not so easily be lost to the vagueness. Still, I searched.

Disappointment threatens the gate of my ch'ulel, but I sit up—leveling the harsh vertical horizon back to its proper orient—not allowing such an intruder too near me. I take the hours glowing air into my lungs and stand, spreading my arms and legs to shake the night from them before heading inside for morning with Mother and Father. We share mash and roots together. I ask them if they had any grand visits while they dreamt, but they did not; however, Father says, "Skybreaker is in slumber now, Daughter. He needs to preserve and store his power for the eclipse."

"The moon moves fast. He will be upon us, and you shall see him again soon," adds Mother.

"When is soon? Balam is on hunt again. They must make it back."

Father clasps my shoulder as we sit in circle. "You sleep

two more nights, Cualli. Then, we ritual under the moon and sun while they are together above us. It is then we will bleed and pour ourselves for the Breaker of Skies."

43

CHAPTER EIGHT

Lands, oceans, mountains, and skies . . . are all left to waste in Cualli's dream. She stirs in her sleep with shallow moans sounding more like whimpers, letting go of the turmoil she's witnessing. A foreboding sky roils with dark, smoke-colored wisps that sail themselves across the vastness under a solid onyx shell that has encased the planet in entirety. The dark smoke whirls overhead, riding atmosphere currents like abyssal dragons—dragons made of the blackest ash one can imagine, the type of ash that could only be from the vilest of throats. All light has ceased from the peninsula Cualli calls home. The jet-black shell over the Earth shields the ash, heat, anguish, and death within so none of it is to escape; it's all left to devour and breed and grow and spread and end all else. The dense forestation has gone from green to muted tones of melancholy.

A rodent scurries the ashen floor far more slowly than it used to. One of its hind legs drags, leaving a pattern in the fallout of ash similar to that of a snake pushing itself through the muted damnation. The rodent's nose has stopped its twitching by now, the heavy acrid air having burned the lining of the two passages. The search for food has been given up on, though, it continues dragging its leg through the soot in hopes of a small basin of water. But what water will it find? It continues the slogged journey only to hear the splintering of one of the few leafless trees that still stands. The dehydrated bark and limbs so overburdened with the weight of ash collecting over and over in caked layers that it can hold no more, snapping and dropping to the grave of the ground below—crushing the rodent. The debris severs its thin little spine much as the ash had forced the separation of the tree's limb.

Jaguar's ears perch themselves higher, noting the thud in the distance that followed crisp sounds of kindled wood splitting, her eyes not eager enough to check the direction for safety; she is tired, exhausted. Eventually, Jaguar reaches a small basin of pooled water. Having trekked for days under the darkness above her jaw is slack and tongue dry as sun-bleached bone. Her firm pad of nostrils leans down, taking in the scent of the water which is grey with murk, and her brow sinks further with a sense of somber defeat, causing her large once brilliantly aware eyes to become less round.

The pool smells of brimstone and looks like spilled paint.

She leans farther, taking a lap with her pale pink tongue while her brow sits heavy and dour. Grey milk hangs from the hooks that pattern her tongue. It burns. Stings. The basin's acidity takes advantage of her cracked and parched mouth, leaving her wincing and shaking the poison from herself.

Jaguar turns.

Shoulders sloughed; tops of paws dragging on her leave.

Her journey doesn't take her elsewhere. She lies herself on her side but ten yards from the basin's shore, the brimstone snow sticking to her fur like marsh cat-tail fluff clinging to a water's edge.

Jaguar commits to her expiration.

The land the Maya have called home since their beginning of time will continue to diminish until all that's left is the purest form of nothing. Even the cracked clay of the barren has turned in this nightmare-scape of Cualli's. Where before the sun would shine down, painting the barren with a warm taupe—tinged orange on the hottest of days—it is now colorless. Silent. And only the permeated odors of rotten death and ashen fire meander slightly from the stagnancy.

The pyramid that stood in the barren is but a scorched and destroyed ruin, smothered in black dust amassed so high it appears as a fallen place of power floating in a lake of mud—a barren of quicksand colored like pitch.

Some of the bird life that too shared this land has made for the skies. Hoping that distance will bring them an escape from the dense shell above that took away the light of day. West they go, until their wings can take them no more.

They rest and even find clear water at first; then, they dart north . . . reaching for higher latitude, still in the search for a new day—the current night and swallowed sky lasting far too long.

Knowing some seasons are harsher than others, their wills remain strong. But after they reach the northern land where buffalo replace tapir and mountain lions climb trees rather than jaguars, it's clear that it's not a matter of distance that will save them from the suffocating shell enclosing them in Hell's furnace. The onyx sky reaches forever. The blockage of any semblance of day is absolute. And by the time this realization is within grasp under the bone caps of their feathered skulls, the reaper is upon them . . . ready for the harvest of their fluttering souls. Their breaths are labored; the atmosphere is saturated with infernal smoke, and their silken lungs are overburdened filters, drenched in blood-soaked ash.

The dying birds lie on their sides like no bird ever should. Mahogany-red bubbles roll from their beaks, and their last breaths are inhaled by the reaper standing ambitiously over them.

Not much farther north, a leaf from a late summer milkweed droops. It is an emerald-green plate covered by an immense serving of fallen carbon atop—appearing as an early covering of dirty snow. Soon enough, the leaf sours, soaking up that which has fallen as though it is the victim of a cruel act . . . The torture forced. It is drowning, the gemlike color taken from it, evaporated into the dryness. The plant does all it knows; it gives up the once-green plate and the many others it held so dear, all falling to the infernal winter's ground. This milkweed hadn't yet flowered to do its part in helping seed the land for next year's royal butterflies. So, it hopes to make a hasty recovery and will let its stretch to the now darkened skies wilt and die; it will pour its last stored energy into its roots, its heart. That is all it knows to do. Its ancestors have passed down such guidance. Dormancy under the ground, that is the plan until the sense of clear, bright skies can be felt emanating from above, then, one last final stretch to the heavens in a hurry to throw a majestic flower—a late-season hope.

Just a hope. Nothing more.

Grasses and plants have browned and fallen everywhere paws could step and eyes could peep. With no sun to bathe in and rain only of liquid carbon—a cocktail for demons and devils—all life shudders before a final fall.

Cualli winces—still asleep but hoping to wake—as she sees even the denizens of the dirt suffering. Worms near the milk-weed's root can't escape the cremation from above; what liquid does fall from the dark clouds still has to seep somewhere after it lands. Bees have nothing to collect but their dehydrated and dead scouts. They carry the corpses back to their honeycombed graveyard, feeling it better to perish together, the hive refusing to give up their strength of community. Beetles have nothing more to crunch than sideways birds and carcasses of deer that go unrotting. The greyness covers everything and staunches even the infinitesimal life that would love nothing more than to devour, multiply, and distend stomachs of the dead until climactic bursts.

A heavy foot fall crashes in the distance. Cualli feels a wave of pressure and sees the surrounding ash vibrate with a quick shake—sending the grey blanket into a settle an inch lower than it was. There's something drastic about this distant rumble, unsettling, giving start to an eagerness laced with stomach-churning anxiety.

Cualli senses no land is safe.

She bounds for an ocean.

Her dreaming mind has an expectation of salted breezes, rushes of cool mist thrown from frothy white capped waves, stray gulls riding the openness of empty oceanic skies, blank horizons, and perhaps even gentle moans from narrowly heard whales far in the blue. These expectations are disemboweled. The breeze is hot; the mist is not thrown from waves but vomited in a spray from boiling soup that extends as far as any eye could see. The water is the color of a thousand crushed salmon—a roiling strawberry pool with a temperature to melt skin, muscle, and sinew . . . leaving bone to float then dive on a whim. The surface of the reddened ocean looks as though there's a torrential downpour, an incessant pelting of rain disrupting the water's grace into a simmering frenzy. The oceans have too been betrayed. The onyx shell is a watchful, contemptuous eye above, holding all the hell within.

Another heavy foot fall and a roar buckles the sound of torrid ocean spray, leaving only a clap of thunderous rage across the vastness.

The guttural rage rumbles on, seemingly unending and gaining ground. It echoes across the damned atmosphere murderously, bringing the water to boil even harder. Foot falls become heavier. Faster. Closer. There is an apprehensive insecurity in the thunderous growling rage . . .

. . . Something has been seen that cannot be left or allowed to be remembered.

A vile jaw collapses around Cualli's dreamscape. Sundering the link. Fracturing whatever memory may have sought to hold on.

CHAPTER NINE

Warriors

The group of hunters well within the west jungle, past the fields, move slowly yet steadily, their eyes and ears as keen as a quetzal searching for a mate. The Yucatan jungle is thick and unforgiving. New people to this land would either turn back—thinking the landscape impenetrable—or force their march through with the aid of destructive engines. Even roaring monsters of the white man's design would find the task troublesome, choking on the dense vines and lush drapery.

Balam, Aapo, and the others are practiced though and have been for many Maya suns. Even at their youngest, the Yucatan engulfed them as they played and got lost in the thickets, their little bodies small enough to venture within the maze like native rodents. As the years increased, so too did the boys' understanding of the living, breathing jungle, making their expertise come with perfect timing for their strong adult forms. Where most men would be struck with awe and impossibility when faced with the peninsula's thickest habitat, these young adult Maya hunters find themselves in the comfort of their home where they are kings, alongside the jaguar and weaving serpents. They sluice through underbrush as thorny and green as the lashes saddled over a tree viper's eyes. They slip over entanglements of roots like the heavy rains from the heavens. They trudge efficiently and silently through mud pools and shallow quicksand like worms channeling through weights of rainforest decay.

Currently, they near the pinnacle of their skills, and their practiced advance of death arrows and stone-bladed axes continue patiently onward through the dense, humid jungle until they see Balam's and Aapo's hands steady themselves. Their arrows nock bow strings, and their feet match the stillness of nearby trunks. Further silence somehow falls over them, as if a misty fog of muteness is gifted from Mother Earth.

Leaves crisp and depress in the sodden floor ahead. Balam looks back to Aapo and the others, mouthing, "Tapir."

The mammal makes its way through the thick fence of shrub and trees that shield it from Balam and Aapo's force of hunters. Aapo slowly lofts a single finger in the humid air signaling his question to his warrior brethren. Balam nods with the same speed, affirming the number of beasts ahead. They remain as still as a patient spider watching in silent anticipation while its prey advances the mine field of natural order. Its elongated snout grasps greens to eat with each leisurely step through what it feels is a thicket of safety. No predators here. A free roam area nestled in the jungle, here for the mammals who need such a place.

A softened branch loosened months ago by a strong storm of heavy winds and torrential downpour becomes two under the herbivore's four-toed hoof. The sound is more of a thud than a snap, as if a small fruit fell to the moist leaf littered floor—water isn't just life here, it's silence that contributes to stealth, aiding the chance at life, but too death. Shallow and steady breaths from the Maya hunters lead to an opportunity through a narrow window in the fence of vertical growth. When the tapir's front quarter enters the opportunistic space between pillars, Balam gives a light grunt sounding much like a deer's bleat, bringing an abrupt end to the tapir's casual disposition and mistaken thought of safety. Its head is thrown the direction of the bleat, its elongated snout hanging in sway. Unblinking, beady eyes are wide in focus on both sides of this battle for survival—predator and prey.

The anxious stillness upon the jungle is palpable. Bow strings are held taught after being strategically drawn on Balam's grunt to stop the tapir inside of the thicket's window; sweat beads on brows and ends of noses, daring to distract the hunters from their aim and focus. The tapir wrestles with the choice to remain silent and still—to passively evade—or to mad dash—to not stick around to find out if there's merely a neighboring deer nearby, or something more sinister at work.

The stare-off, the pooling sweat, the pulsing anxiety, all hangs thick in the air. Hearts are felt in throats.

As if there is a sixth sense, the language of one of their gods perhaps, the Maya hunters loose their grip, allowing bow strings to roll off briny fingertips. Arrows fly. Cries and whistles of death penetrate the stale air and a rush of wind where there was none before births from the fright of birds leaving their stoops.

Balam and Aapo lax their weapons to their side as the others rush in with stampeding foot falls of calloused, golden-brown heels. Trusting their stone hammers and obsidian-bladed axes more than the new and still fairly unfamiliar ranged choice of bow and arrow, they bludgeon the dropped tapir into a fast and final restful end.

Aapo looks to Balam with a keen smirk. "I dressed the last one, Brother. Your turn to get dirty."

A firm hand smacks Aapo's shoulder with a held grip. If there were any birds still residing in the canopy, they would be setting their wings to the sky upon hearing the deeply whole laugh from Balam's chest. "This is truth," he says, laughing more and matching Aapo's grin. "Hold my bow."

A campfire crackles and scorns the night's damp air, fighting no longer to take hold of its fuel of deadfall. It has won the battle this night thanks to the help from the Maya hunters. They sit, most of them in a misshapen circle around the angry flames, pulling meat from bone, eating and sharing stories together. Some are in whispers; others exclaim and gesture to aid in their grandiose tale. Balam and Aapo thought it best to set up for a night in the thicket, being that they had traveled far enough into the jungle that they would not have made it back home before dusk—the weight and extra work of the tapir hindering their speed. The one hind quarter they eat under the starlit skies will only make tomorrow's trek back that much easier. Balam and Aapo agreed as one that the men deserved a restful and enjoyable night sharing tales and jests together.

The two leaders sit together away from their group of men, eating alone and watching the comradery out of sight—within the shadows—only rarely being licked by the infernal flicker.

"She's on your mind," says Aapo.

Balam shoots a quick exhale out his nose. "And how would you know that, Brother?"

"You're quiet, and that meat grows cold. It is either her or the Skybreaker perhaps that takes your thoughts." Aapo raises a bone that's nearly all gristle and fat but finds one more bite worth taking. "My bet is on her though. Is it not truth?" he asks, chewing at the same time.

Balam raises the chunk of tapir meat held in his hand. "You're right. My evening meal has grown cold while she races through my thoughts. It's not a bad thing, Brother, just something I can't help. She comes and she goes as she pleases, much like the clouds."

"Are you going to eat it?"

Balam laughs from his nose again, looking to Aapo. His eyes leave the hot orange dance between his men for the first time since they sat down. "You need it far more than me! Skinny shit."

Aapo tosses his well-cleaned bone into the maze of forest

and catches the thrown chunk of meat, all in a single dexterous manner, offering nothing but a nod and snigger.

"What of it anyways?" Balam says after a moment of silence between them.

"Huh?" Aapo's brow furls in confusion as Balam's question catches him off-guard—mid-bite and distracted. "Oh, Cualli?" He catches on.

"Yeah, what of it? You bring it up as though you're mocking or thinking me misguided."

Aapo swallows hard. Maybe in a fast bought of stirs, as if anxiety is hitting him like a brisk night wind. Or to simply clear his mouth. More than likely though, both. He lets his hands take rest on his knees, adopting a genuine and more serious look than he had before when the conversation had hints of jest and sarcasm—a common air the two have grown to admire and expect from each other. Although they are not fully aware of it, this behavior of throwing harmless spears at each other is a sign of how their trust has grown over the years, at times, throwing spears laced with words most others would deem as poisonous, but between these two, who have hunted and battled the elements for so long together, the poison only brings forth laughs and a deeper, entwining bond.

"I only mean that you could have any of our women back home and even pick from the ones a few years past Cualli. We have lots of strong women, some that would challenge you. And your heart.

"I only mean, you're our best hunter, Brother. Becoming

one of our leading Elders later in life is a sight I'll likely see within my own."

There is pause between them. They hear neither the screaming logs under the fire nor the stories being told within the orange dance. Even the tales reaching crescendo are lost to them. They each understand the gravity that's been created. Balam quietly tries to understand Aapo's view and direction in silence while too looking to choose his words with wisdom, not wishing to bring on a battle of defensiveness between them. Aapo continues to make progress on the last bit of food, internally hoping a line hasn't been crossed; he means well and fears any war that would rift the earth between his Maya brother and himself.

"I cannot say it with any strong explanation, Aapo. There aren't words for the truth I try to say. She slows the wind around me, letting me see our world, the Mother Earth, more clearly than before. I even see myself more clearly when she's near. None of our other women have shown me that."

Aapo sits up straighter with a weighty breath. "I think you've spoken a more clear truth than you've given yourself credit for. I cannot say I understand, but I can say that if any of our women gave me whatever it is you just spoke of, I trust my decision would be just as easily made."

Balam looks to his most trusted brother and nods in a simple but stern and respectful bow. "Thanks, Brother."

"You have my apology for bringing it up. I have no reason to doubt your judgments. I meant no bad season between us."

"The apology is neither accepted nor needed. I only ever ask of you to speak your mind, speak truth to me, and do so without the worry. There may be times when I am missing something that you may see with a clearer eye. This is why you must speak unhindered."

"Because you could be wrong. Got it."

"Ha! Exactly, but do not ever count on it too much," Balam says with a lace of familiar—harmless—poison. "Cualli is strong, Brother. She may be small and not as seen in crowds like some of the others who travel our lands in packs, rarely leaving each other's sides, but that is something I like. Cualli is strong in heart, around me even more so, and she isn't loud and squealy like the others." Balam grunts in disapproval. "I hate it when they get loud. Pains my ears. I'd rather be dragged up a tree by a big cat."

"I like it when they're loud . . ."

The volume in the air picks up with a sudden bought of bellows from their chests while Aapo chucks the remains of Balam's dinner off into the darkness, and so unabatedly the others hear them for the first time over their ruckus around the hearth.

"Yeah, you do like the loud ones," says Balam, laughs still echoing the air. "And most of them you've tainted already with your small manhood—"

"Hey!"

"—and I don't want anything you've been inside already. Which doesn't leave much, does it?"

"Harsh, Brother, harsh," Aapo says dryly.

The two Maya warriors glance each other out the corners of their eyes, giving a moments silence before again drowning out the comradery around the fire in the distance and the cacophony of nocturnal insects surrounding the chill darkness with their barrage of mirth.

With the fire down, only holding onto life by a couple struggling embers exhaling smoke that barely survives as it reaches the edge of the canopy, a much quieter air than last night's rolls among the band of hunters. The keen attention they paid to stories told, the excitement and loud voices shared together, the energy exuded in their different manners of participation, has all led to a mutual and unspoken desire—a need even—for a calm after the storm, a soft morning of recharge from the vast extroversion. In this quiet, however, they keep steadily busy, quartering what remains of the tapir, gathering up tools and packs they had brought with on their hunt which they had planned for possibly taking up to three times longer than it had, and cutting down several saplings—young and green—to work well for tying together the quartered harvest and using their strength in numbers to carry the animal's weight on poles across their shoulders.

They kick out the last struggling embers and make their journey back home to their people, who are busy keeping up with their own contributions to the tribe, trusting but hoping though too, that Balam, Aapo, and the others have succeeded in their part to bring back enough kill for a grand feast in the coming days before the celestial event—a feast that will surely be celebrated as another gesture of their gratitude and worship to the Skybreaker.

And a grand feast it is.

On their return, celebration ensues. Those that were on the hunt deep in the western jungle sit cross-legged while some of the tribe's elder women paint their faces, decorating them as they truly are—as hunters and warriors—so all their people can see success, power, and status across their faces. Reds, white, and rich black are used. Red to show that blood has been spilled. White shows that the sun god shines bright on their ch'ulels. And black signifies their strength to take life from the jungle so it can then give life to their people, even those unable to hunt for themselves. Black, for masters of both life and death and givers to their people. Balam stands, having his warrior's paint done by a proud mother of four, a woman in her fifth decade of life with inked skin and piercings to show for her many years. Her stretched lobes no longer hold stone but wood, as her failing and sagging skin no longer does well with the weight of heavier jewelry. She is proud of her art across the young man's face and the opportunity to make him look striking and powerful to all the onlooking eyes as he thrusts his fists to the sky.

He can see the amount of black paint covering his nose and

cheekbones. He can feel the confidence seep into him—from the paint as well as the ruckus of his Maya people exclaiming while he holds his fists high.

"For you all! And for the Breaker of Skies!" shouts Balam, trying to boast his voice over the others who are showing their praise by calling out his, Aapo's and the other's names.

Dances and games fill the land when bellies can hold no more. Sweat glistens on golden skin in the hours of sun and on into dusk, where the astral temperature radiates to Earth, chilling salted epidermis to a comfortable calm.

Cualli watches Balam from afar as he attempts several times to escape what has been constant attention since their latest return from the west. She finds humor in it as much as she finds a longing for his success. Her vision goes past the paint—that is mostly black and powerful—and sees a man who she believes is nothing less than a leader. A mortal with a grand heart that not only beats for himself, but also his Maya people. And . . . for her, she hopes.

As the blue-tinted landscape turns to opaque dullness, most of the celebration gathers nearest a large pit of open flame. Many of the silhouettes within the bubble of warm light request the tale of the hunt be told to their curious ears. They do not say it, but they wish for their ears to hear something extravagant, nearing the unbelievable, even if it means that truth will be bent in doing so. As this goes unsaid, so too does the hunters' understanding of what the pleading tribesmen and women desire, and how when they tell their tale it will be just that. A tale, a tall tale. One that will be as grand to tell as it will be to hear.

Cualli stays clear of the emanating firelight as the inside of her chest leads her feet around the mass of voices. She easily goes unseen and finds Balam who has finally found his peace in darkness, where even hot serpent tongues fail to lick as they lash out like whips from the hellish pit. A nod from Balam helps a smile crack the deep shadow in which they stand. Cualli's sign of happiness is the only light this far from the glowing orb they've both left.

She takes a stance next to him, on his right side, their gazes set the same—simply observing the gathering commune as the mess of voices hushes ever so slightly, a tall tale beginning.

A silence remains between them, one that nudges Balam with an initial unease, provoking him to speak up. He does not wish to make his Cualli feel uncomfortable or ignored. "It is good to see you, Cualli. Tell me of your day."

"You have spoken enough today," says Cualli. "Let us simply be. Here. Standing together."

Balam is unsure—confused—at first and struck with a surprise he has not found himself in before. He looks to Cualli, searching for an understanding on her face even in the dark air. His look goes unmet, her direction still towards their Maya people, though the side of her face is enough for Balam to reach the understanding he seeks. Her gentle and kind disposition taking his hand, leading him to see that she knows why he is alone, away from the others. Her true contentedness is simply in being here, together in silence, while still knowing everything is ok. Nothing is wrong.

His face shows his feelings as he joins Cualli in looking back ahead. Too far away is the gathering to hear details other than that, it's clearly several different voices telling the tale back and forth, and occasional gasps that permeate the night in unison. The two feel safe in the quietness they've created together. A safety that feels like solitude to them both, even though their number is two.

CHAPTER TEN

Guile can feel the approach. Hundreds, then thousands. Each footstep a dot on the dark god's radar, inching along like a swarm of hurried insects to a decaying carcass. Pulled by the desire for survival, not knowing of the insidious plague the carcass contains.

His breathing is shallow, unexcitable, patient. Eyes still closed, and heart nothing but faint not often thrums.

CHAPTER ELEVEN

Cualli

With my witz pendant now in hand, I pounce through the entrance of our home to catch back up to Mother and Father, tying the necklace as I run. The sun is high and hot this day, and the moon is barely visible on its approach in the infernally illuminated sky.

"Mother, Father," I say in gasp, taking a moment to catch my breath. "We are not to be late, are we?"

Father points to the orb with the more rapid orbit closing its gap to the sun. "There is still time, more time than is needed for us to reach the barren." He laughs with a shake of his head. "Breathe, Cualli."

The moon must appear to move across the heavens faster for me than for Father—deceiving me. The speed of the celestial body races in my gut; I too feel it in my wrists, my pulse heavy as we near the temple. Our tribe is seen ahead of us, beside us, behind us. We are all on the same path to the barren ground that surrounds the foot of the pyramid. The same place Skybreaker placed me after pulling me to his plane. The same place Balam and I chose our cutting stones. There are mothers holding their children much too young to walk the distance. There are of-age men and women helping our elderly make the walk—taking their arms and supporting their shoulders. There are peers of mine, those not yet of age but needed for this grand event. There are our mighty and strong hunters and warriors in their smaller groups all around, loudly singing songs of heart and courage, songs of blood.

As we finally near our destination after the hefty trek, all our Elders are seen ahead at the center of the taupe-scaled landscape. The tall step pyramid that is the Kan Temple stands, grand and beautiful, behind them. And there is the moon, high in the incendiary sky; much closer now, threatening the sun with its coming intent to block its life from us.

I see Balam through the crowd off to my right, he leads Aapo and the others. I cast him a gentle smile, and his return settles the churning world in my stomach and anxious blood in my veins. My moistened feet from the lush, green land we've traveled to get here are now dusted with the dry powder of clay that lies atop the cracked surface. I look up. This area of dead land around the pyramid acts as a window to the mass vista of sky, making the heavens appear even grander . . . It's like traveling to another plane. If it were not for my feet, I'd believe myself flying the endlessness beyond the astral gates.

"We must go ahead now, Cualli," says Mother as she gives my shoulder a sign that she cares.

"What? Why?" I say. "Are we not to be together for this?"

Father draws the shape of a triangle fan on his palm with

his finger and taps at the center of the invisible shape where its width is shortest. "We always take mass ritual with those oldest in suns at the front. You, Cualli, will be back here." He taps his finger on his palm again, showing a rough location. "And our youngest Maya hearts will be further back yet. Here.

"We fan out by age. You will be amongst your peers. It is where you are most needed—in your proper place within the line of blood power."

"But what of those less than two suns?" I understand Father, but I am also surprised. I both expected and wanted to be with my family. In this moment, the skies cloud ever so slightly in my chest; my shoulders are not as sharp and tall as moments before.

Mother speaks, "Those who cannot leave their mothers are to be with them, and their mothers will be the ones to spill their blood along with their own. The only exception is for our babes, Cualli. Father speaks truth."

She takes my hands, enveloping them in front of me. "We are so proud of you." She grips my hands more tightly. "Be strong. Bleed well. We will see you after Skybreaker pushes the moon. Okay?"

I look to Father. His face is stern, lips pursed in a familiar look that tells me to be strong, to believe, and to hold myself with pride.

"Okay." I nod—pursing my own lips, my brow following suit to match my father's.

They head on towards their place in the fan shape we are to make, and I soon lose them in the sea of our tribe.

For some time, the barren is in a type of organized chaos while we find our places and help others find theirs. Our voices echo throughout, blotting out any natural ambient sounds that would waft across the barren circle. I settle into where, I believe, my place is in the line of blood power. My peers are all around, and I can just barely make out Balam in the lines ahead with Aapo. We are the same age. We could take place next to each other. I could move up and be with him and Aapo . . .

I start to move forward, giving in to the buildup of desire. On my very first step, though, I hear one of our Elders who I cannot see—as they are so far ahead and blocked by the ocean of my fellow Maya—call out to all of us. "Let us bring our knees to the Mother Earth. Let us give our eyes to the clay." His strained voice cuts the hot air, bringing a sudden and absolute silence.

In this moment of communal quiet I start to see the bodies ahead of me lower themselves to the ground, to their knees. It comes as a giant wave, taking those ahead of Balam before taking him; those between us follow, and the wave takes me too. All my peers, left and right, kneel to the ground with me. I see them and the thousand Maya souls ahead bow, taking their eyes down close to the ground. I do the same, though I feel like I am the last to do so; my young child-like heart wants to take it in. I want to see it all—all our mass numbers bowed low to the clay in unison. I want to witness everything of my first ritual with my people.

All I see now is the warm, cracked clay and the shadows

of those at my sides. The air is still, and the silence remains. I hear my breathing and too the breaths of those most near. The air I exhale hits the earth, sending orange dust into a flight that almost settles before the next small gust breaks it from the scaled land again. I do not know what is to come next. I am in nerves and reach to my tapir-skin pouch for my blue-edged stone; I hold it tightly in my sweating hand. Something assails the air ahead, near the front and those who are oldest. It comes as another wave, riding the line of blood power by age. As my ears open for an answer, as the wave speeds to crash the shore of me and those my age, I hear it. A heavy and proud chant rides this air. And now, I am calling it as well.

Within seconds, I can hear those younger, behind me, calling it too.

Tal- . . . Tal- . . . Tal- . . .

Our chant thickens as we vocalize, the ground our faces are so near acting as instrument.

Tal- . . . Tal- . . . Tal- . . .

Our voices crowd and displace the atmosphere. I can feel the volume and power of our words in my chest; the barren where we kneel now feels like a drum.

Tal- . . . Tal- . . . Tal- . . .

Tal- . . . Tal-Tz'ay . . . Tal-Tz'ay . . .

All together, we are saying, "Come, come down." As we chant, the air starts to chill the tops of my shoulders, my bare back, the nape of my neck. Like an unheard breeze preluding a stormfront, it brings tiny bumps of cold across me as the shadows of my peers fade. As my shadow fades. As the day itself fades, leaving us in torrential dusk. The moon has taken its stance.

Something stirs the ground at the front of the fan. Another wave, this one is felt more than heard. And it comes with haste! As my eyes view the now darkened ground, my fist—along with a thousand others—hits the drum to the timing of our constant song to the Skybreaker.

Tal- . . . Tz'ay- . . . Kan- . . . Kan-Koj . . .

We repeat and beat at the drum of the Mother, the drum of the Earth.

Our Elders call—yell—out for us to bleed for the Breaker of Skies. The beating of the drum ceases, and I drag the gorgeous blue blade across my left wrist. I drag it slowly, and I put it deep, and true! Even though the barren is filled with the storm of our call to the god, I still hear the thin flesh of my inner wrist peel and tear apart as the sharpness of my cutting stone breaks the taught tension that kept the shell of my daint wrist together and whole.

There is no pain; my nerves take care of that. Only a deep maroon spill of life blood seeps out to the dry, dusty clay. I cannot take my eyes from it—the blood. It is life. It is beauty. It is power. I drag the blue edge across again, for we must give enough to him if he is to move the moon. And I will give all I can. This time a sharp spark flies up into my elbow, the pain riding a tendon. I wince not, for this is a spark to relish. I must do my part, and I must be proud.

The beating of the drum starts again. My bloody fist contributes as I call out with the others in chant, louder than before. And I watch as the ground before me soaks with my blood, pouring into the cracks of the scorched barren, down into the world's core.

Tal- . . . Tz'ay- . . . Kan- . . . Kan-Koj . . .

Tal- . . . Tz'ay- . . . Kan- . . . Kan-Koj . . .

Come . . . Down . . . Sky . . . Skybreaker . . .

The ground shakes. With a power so vast it cannot be from the beating of our bloody fists. It reverberates through the floor where I kneel. Is this another wave? What comes next . . .

But the quake in the ground does not come like the other waves; it is getting stronger but unmoving, this wave is not coming back to us . . .

. . . A single scream sounds, then—screams. Screams that are nearly drowned out from the drum and the song. The rumble and quake do not cease but grow. Something is wrong. The moon still shades us; our drum starts to quiet. I bring my face up from the sodden red clay. The sky is dark! Some are running from the front of the line of power; the ground now feels as though it is going to break, my knees rattling with pain from the tremors.

Others around me and ahead are too looking up, having stopped their calls to the god. The shaking of the very earth grows and grows, and erupts at the base of the fan, throwing massive pieces of the ground along with many bodies through the air. A stone titan pushes itself out of the barren with its gargantuan head and maw thrown to the sky as it roars a song so loud and vast the pressure on my ears pounds as if a boulder has fallen, crushing my head.

My eyes shut hard, and I try to give my ears an escape from the sound of war. The eruption of stone continues as the dripping, saliva-filled cavern of the colossal god's mouth thrashes and speaks its abyssal volumes. The ground quakes and bursts larger, making more and more room for the sand-colored, rotund dragon's emergence. Chaos reigns all around. The air holds no room for the screams of our tribe to be heard as it is overtaken by the immense sound of cracking earth and power from the god's monstrous jaw.

I don't know what is happening . . . and I am frozen in place. Our people are running and shrieking for their children and families, but I can do nothing but stare and watch as my tribe is crushed under massive reptilian paws and slung through the air by huge, scaled wings that thrust through the smattering of ants that we all now are.

The dark god's eyes open with the resonant pounding of fists on his ceiling of sun-baked clay and stone. His shoulders give a slight roll—the first movement the Dark One has made in eons—and a deep breath of his curdles within his wide saurian throat. For the first time since the last scourge, his patience is allowed to step aside, giving way for the dry, ancient, stagnant air in his earthen casket to birth excitement into his filling lungs.

Guile sends a beckoning presence to the Elders kneeling and chanting above him. A mental persuasion—a call both vile and divine—that now is the time for a lake of blood to spread across the barren. Under the cool shade of the moon, each Elder hears what they believe is the Skybreaker reaching out for them, asking their tribe to make a grand offering, so he may gain enough power to take flight and break the sinister moon away from its stubborn station affront the sun.

The beating upon Guile's ceiling stops, and the scent of iron fills his nose, bringing the thick scales across the dark god's reptilian jowls to quiver in a tremorous lust. An ancient, evil thirst takes over and drives Guile to satiate his yearning for everbearing darkness and apocalyptic demise of all, for his solitude and supremacy to reign once again. The rain from their wrists seeps through the cracked terrain, a flood over a drain that soon reaches Guile's chamber of rest, bathing him in the power he needs. The tin-like clinking of red droplets on armored scales sounds in his casket like piano keys dancing in staccato—a most ominous tune, fit for bringing about the end of days.

The crust underfoot the Elders quakes as the dark god's emergence threatens. Thoughts of question and intrigue pique their minds; they wonder if the skies resonate with such force that the barren itself feels the power of the Skybreaker's beating wings. Cause for alarm speaks in volumes though, as the concussive quakes only escalate, ramping up quickly and shaking the earth so violently that the seven most decorated Maya are forced to stand, escaping the pain in their knees from the dense clay grating at their skin like a saw teases first the bark of a tree. Foreshocks reach from the now bursting crust at the epicenter of the cause. Where once the Elders stood, the ground cracks and shelves, whipping the air with the harshest of low shattering sounds—death cries of the planet. This displaces more Maya people, those nearest the front of the fan shape quickly stand and move away, bumping into those still on their knees whose confusion has only begun to set. The jutting clay and stone rises, and rises, and spreads, spreading into a chasm as otherworldly, saurian roars escape from the depths.

With finality, Guile thrusts forth from the jagged hole in the barren, throwing mass lobs of the cracked earth into the air, smashing bodies into the ground as they settle from their given flight. Seeing, hearing—witnessing—the dark god's partial emergence, all but one of the Yucatan's Maya rise in attempt to flee or search for loved ones. They scream and yelp in torrents of magnificent despair as chaos floods their brains. Their cries, if they could be heard over the dark god and crust of the Earth's own mammoth orchestral song-of-end, would be a sound so sour and horrific it would bring any living soul's face to streak with salted water, and their hearts to become contents of their stomach, like heavy sunken anchors of ships long lost to demise at sea.

Guile lumbers out of the massive chasm that is now a full

rift in the clay wasteland, clawed hands first meeting bodies rather than stone. Flesh, blood, guts, and bone slew into the cracks of the scorched barren like grout being troweled across a finely laid stone floor—Cualli's people becoming one with the Earth. He throws his head high to the sky in triumph, once more letting out a curdling roar that sends cracks through the ominous, shielded sky. White splints like lightning shatter out from the space where the moon has chosen its seat in front of the infernal sun, cracking the blackened sky. The white, jagged cuts across the heavens dissolve to darkness, matching again the opaque death from the moon. What's left behind is nothing but the grey stone moon and an infinite black sea—spread wide and endless. Cualli sees it as a solid slab of obsidian overhead. The end of light.

As the dark god's bark of gravelly, throaty, disdainful command to the moon trails to an end, the moon will no longer move.

It must obey now that Guile has shattered the sky, turning it solid and forever. The moon is forced to accept its seat in the obsidian sea.

Now that he has killed the sky and wrought the Earth with everbearing shadow, the dark god tromps through Maya by the dozens. The hundreds. Each step the towering colossus takes ends the beating of desperate hearts. And his steps, they do not cease . . .

Bounding a different direction with every ceaseless, murderous step and genocidal collapsing of his epochal jaws, Guile dominates what is now nothing but clay waste. The dark god thrashes his rust-colored scaled wings and body around the open field, ripping through and smashing down Maya lives, roaring as he does in insatiable thirst, all while adorned in an ever-flowing bath of glistening cherry. The barren is a field of decimation. His vile mouth drips with flesh and flood waters worth of red. As he churns bodies, ear-shattering, ungodly roars rupture the atmosphere, spraying gristle across the clay plain of disgust that was once a simple and sanctified barren.

The spray looks like fog from where Cualli stands, but she knows the sorrowful truth . . . that the mist is more than bestial salivation.

It turns her cold.

She feels as if all moisture has left not only her sweet lips and her throat, but even her lungs and soul feel desert dry. Her knees remain set like stone on what is no longer the homeland that she has known all her life. She cannot move! She can feel in her heart that she wants to—there is still time and chance to flee. Her courage, what she has sought and worked so hard on, has fled without her though, leaving her behind. All the work, all the conflict, all the lack of confidence and unsureness—or self-power as she calls it—that she turned into conviction and driving force, all the growth . . . adulthood, that she so often found herself crying for within. All the time spent on her witz jade—tearing the very fibers and tendons in her hands—to materialize, ritualize, and manifest the hard-boned courage she put above almost all else. To now have it all flee—without her.

Tragedy.

She brings her hand up, gripping the jade glyph, wishing she felt deserving of wearing such a symbol. Wetness runs from her ears, dripping to her neck and pooling in the cradles of her soft collarbones. While her blank gaze is set hard ahead at the massacre before her, a familiar figure is noted, catching her attention even among the carnage and terrified screaming people—her people. Even in such chaos, he's hard for her to miss.

Balam.

She feels the continued cadence of red rain droplets on her neck as she sees her warrior running toward her. The dark god—the eater of her people—is a gigantic shadow of damnation towering behind him. A shadow so immense it hides the frozen dot of grey high in the sky above.

His knotted hair of locked spears dances in the blood-tinged air as he jumps over corpses, weaving in and around fellow Maya who attempt their own escape. Balam's eyes are wide with gravity as he rushes for his Cualli, who stares back at him, stunned—the only Maya still kneeling on the ground that is no longer a place of home.

"My Cualli!" His voice is drowned out by the song of the end concussing and displacing the air. Cualli's ruptured and crying ears guess his words more than hear them.

"It IS NOT . . ." Balam makes a leap over a shallow mound of death. "It is not the Breaker of—"

Teeth, fangs, shards the size of a human femur clamp

around Cualli's love—her warrior—and raise him to the air, high off the ground of massacre. A calloused foot up to lower knee, falling, is the last she sees of him.

It feels as if all motion has slowed for her. Balam's lower leg takes near an eternity to finish its fall, disappearing into the gore. The oppressive call of hate forth from Guile's maw after his swallow is only a high-pitched ring to her destroyed ears, and the mist thrown from it moving slow enough to her that she picks out the twinkle of her tribe's jewelry, wettened and sanguine tinged in the dark god's spray. In her state, on her pink knees that have turned stubborn and ceramic as the ground on which they are set, she stares forward unblinking, her hand still clutching the jade necklace. The yells and screams, the epochal roars that are song of death. The crushing of her peoples' bodies under the devil's feet and all other sound that would be heard are silenced, either by the need of her young and fragile mind or the destruction on either side of her head.

She stares forward, her mind as silent as her ears, under the hell sky and overbearing God of Guile before her. And she watches as the gargantuan, clawed hand that's nearest, raises to take its next world-damning, Cualli-damning, step.

Author's Note

Here we are, the "Afterword." As I sit here on my couch, in front of a glass of cranberry juice atop the square coffee table I've had for . . . gosh, nearly twenty years now, two things come to mind—the first being how glad I am the wall of glossy black that is the living room TV, is just that, a wall of glossy black, nothing more. The stare it is giving me feels like one of disapproving coercion, though.

"I'm here to be watched. Can you not see me? I know you can . . ." says the TV.

Fucking screens. As the years pass, my resentment for them grows. It may—could—be the meals served through this device that I truly resent though. Thinking more on it, it's likely both. And thinking even more on it, it's the creators of both that should really be the target of my resentment. And they are. To hell with all three actually. Hello, readers! This is what it looks like when I go on a tangent, "Are you not entertained?" Oh, the irony of such a quote . . .

Ok, seriously, onto the second thing at the forefront of my mind—how to start this post-story drivel. Well, I cannot think of a better way to start than to revisit how it began—with a simple yet potent statement. The power of worship is unprecedented. It is humanity's most sacred, and calamitous creation.

And come to think of it, now that we're here, in the Afterword where I should have some grand exposition about how I feel and what the morality and metaphor for the story is, I find myself at a loss. Because, I've already said it all. You've already read it. And I guess that's a good thing, right? The fact that I am here and at a loss for what else to say, I suppose, means I've succeeded (to some degree at least). I've fictionalized the nonfiction; I've fictionalized my own views, worries, and even a little of my own torment. And even some of my hopes. Maybe that's what is missing in the story . . .

Scratches head

The story doesn't allude to my hopes in a straightforward, in-your-face kind of way. So, there it is. That's what I'll add to this damned Afterword, and it will be short. Ready? Here it is: I hope that this story—one that has played out so many times before—never fucking happens again.

Now onto the important shit. The many people I want to thank.

"Tyler, I'm still here, being ignored."

I look up at the TV—the black screen—with a raised eyebrow, casting the soulless object a glare. One that insinuates: *really?*

"Yes, you are" I answer back. Not audibly, though; that

would be crazy.

I want to thank Steve Stred for reading my original draft of this and giving me a nudge by asking, "Have you tried this story in a different POV?" To which I replied, "No. However, when I got to the end, I realized how I may have messed up, as the ending is so cinematic." A real problem to pull off while in first-person present. But I love the first-person perspective, especially for Cualli because I feel it helps me keep the voice I envisioned for her, and that is incredibly important to me. And I feared jumping between first and third may lose or frustrate the reader. To which Steve said, "You did this in *End Realm*, and it worked."

And just like that, with this realization (and ego boost from Steve), I was able to dive back in and tackle the addition of third person text. So much was added after that quick feedback from the first draft. *Skybreaker* nearly doubled in word count; I ended up adding entire chapters that weren't there prior, simply from enjoying the world and characters so much. It was easy to revisit the text, and I look back on this writing fondly. Thanks a ton, Steve. Your feedback is always thought-provoking without being directional, which allows me to stay at the wheel and remain within my own creativity. A mere nudge, and into the waters I went again.

Brittney Norton was my editor for this one. I had worked with her on some smaller pieces, mostly short stories going out to submission piles, and I knew she would be great for this novella. Brittney, thank you for pointing out all my blunders both small and terrible and for being an absolute joy to work with. Thank you so much.

Thank you, Kayleigh Dobbs, C.M. Forest, Jasmine De La Paz, S.Q. McGrath and Drew Starling, for making time in your reading schedules before *Skybreaker*'s release and for such high praise. I appreciate every one of you and wish you all the success the world has to offer. You are all great writers and, well, to the skies with you!

Thank you, Nicole, for again making the face of my book a work of art in its own right. I adore watching you create and love you more than I can say. Thank you for your love, support, encouragement, and constant shared laughs.

I had the general idea for this story and some of its characters for months before setting pen to paper. Even the idea that this vile god would burst forth from somewhere—wasn't sure where or how. Then, I was listening to *The Browning* on a drive to Madison, WI, and their song "Skybreaker," which I hadn't heard before, came on. While it played, the song evoked a very cinematic scene in my mind. A very powerful scene. One of bloodletting and titanic destruction and immense tragedy. My heart pounded through the whole mental movie, and in the moments after the song ended, I just wanted to be home with my pen and paper. I couldn't get home fast enough. *The Browning*, thank you for invoking such a dreadful scene.

As always, thank you to my mother and father, Theone and Michael Welch, for never stifling my creativity, for never feeding me the whole "you can't do anything with art, it won't get you anywhere" speech. Unfortunately, far too many young humans hear this.

Thanks to my proofreaders for catching some edits that slipped through the cracks, it's always humbling and humorous to see the simple shit my editor and I happen to miss along the way. Michael and Nicole, thank you for reading through one final time, and special thanks to Bonnie, for picking up the job so last minute for me!

Also, I'm sincerely thankful for the support and early reviews I received for my last publication, *End Realm*. Special thanks to Kayleigh at *Happy Goat Horror*, Robin at *Inky Bones Press*, Brittney at *Brit Norton Reads*, Elli and Charisa at *The Dead Readers Society*, Cynthia Plante Nunez, Allena at *Allena in Wonderland*, and Safiya at *Written in the Clay*. I fear I am forgetting so many people and so many inspirations, but this must end; I shan't keep you any longer from your next adventure.

Lastly, though certainly not least, to you, all of you who have made it to the last pages of another creation of mine, thank you for choosing my stories. And please, together, let us stop history from repeating itself.

—Tyler J. Welch

About the Author

When Tyler Welch isn't secluded in his Wisconsin dwelling, he can be found deeply engrossed within captivating forests and fog-smothered marshlands, embracing the depth of the world. It's in these secluded corners where he has found inspiration, developing ways to imbue his writing and photography with a distinctive dark artistic style. His work is unique and enticing, pulling us all to find the haunting secrets hidden within.

He lives with his loving wife and two sons, despises stark cold winters, and is in constant search for immortality.

TYLERJWELCH.COM

www.ingramcontent.com/pod-product-compliance
Lightning Source LLC
Chambersburg PA
CBHW031552310726
48973CB00003B/799